Henry C. Wright

The Natick Resolution

AF130477

Anatiposi

Henry C. Wright

The Natick Resolution

Reprint of the original, first published in 1859.

1st Edition 2023 | ISBN: 978-3-38231-290-9

Anatiposi Verlag is an imprint of Outlook Verlagsgesellschaft mbH.

Verlag (Publisher): Outlook Verlag GmbH, Zeilweg 44, 60439 Frankfurt, Deutschland
Vertretungsberechtigt (Authorized to represent): E. Roepke, Zeilweg 44, 60439 Frankfurt, Deutschland
Druck (Print): Books on Demand GmbH, In de Tarpen 42, 22848 Norderstedt, Deutschland

THE

NATICK RESOLUTION;

OR,

RESISTANCE TO SLAVEHOLDERS

THE RIGHT AND DUTY OF SOUTHERN SLAVES AND NORTHERN FREEMEN.

BY HENRY C. WRIGHT.

" RESISTANCE TO TYRANTS IS OBEDIENCE TO GOD."

BOSTON:
PRINTED FOR THE AUTHOR.
1859.

THE NATICK RESOLUTION.

LETTER TO JOHN BROWN.

NATICK, Mass., Nov. 21st, 1859.

CAPT. JOHN BROWN:

DEAR AND HONORED FRIEND — (for the friend of the slave is my dear and honored friend) — A very large and enthusiastic meeting of the citizens of this town, without regard to political or religious creeds, was held last evening, for the purpose of considering and acting upon the following resolution :—

Whereas, Resistance to tyrants is obedience to God ; therefore,
Resolved, That it is the right and duty of the slaves to resist their masters, and the right and duty of the people of the North o incite them to resistance, and to aid them in it.

This resolution was adopted by the meeting without a dissenting voice. Though a United States Senator (Henry Wilson) and a United States Postmaster were present, yet not a voice was raised against it by them, nor by any one else, nor against the sentiments it contains. The meeting appointed me a committee to forward their resolution to you. In compliance with their request, and with the promptings of my own heart, I forward it.

The resolution, as you will see, simply affirms the right and duty of resistance, not merely to slavery as a principle or an abstraction, but to slaveholders, the living embodiment of slavery. The South embody slavery and resistance to liberty in their whole life. We would arouse the North to embody liberty and resistance to slavery in their whole life. Wherever the people of the South live, whether in domestic, social, ecclesiastical, political or commercial life, they embody *death to liberty*. We would stir up the people of the North to embody *death to slavery* wherever they live. In whatever relations they live, we would incite them to embody liberty as the South does slavery. *Death to slavery* should, and will, ere long, be the watchword of every domestic and social circle, of every political and religious party, and of every literary and commercial establishment, in the North.

The blessings of the God of the oppressed rest upon you! This is the prayer of thousands who have known you for years, and entirely sympathize with you in the one great object of your life — *i. e.*, to arouse this nation to look the sin, the shame and danger of slavery in the face. We have felt the deepest interest in your plans and movements, as we have known and watched them the last four years ; and we have wondered that those who hold to armed resistance to tyrants have not more cheerfully and numerously gathered around your standard of insurrection against slaveholders.

The government and God of this nation daily and hourly proclaim to the people of the North, and to the slaves of the South, their right and duty of armed resistance to slaveholders. You hastened to obey that call to duty made by your country and your God. Virginia herself called you to resist slaveholders, and to free the slaves, by arms and blood, if need be. Why should Virginia hang you? You have only done what she has exhorted you to do from the day of your birth. Why should the North call you a "fanatic," a "maniac," a "ruffian," a "marauder," a "murderer," an "assassin"? You have only done what the religion, the government and God of the nation, for seventy years, proclaimed to be your right and your duty.

Twelve days hence, Virginia will hang your body, but she will not hang John Brown. Better to die a traitor to Virginia, than to live a traitor to yourself and your God. This nation of twenty-five millions will kill your body for treason against them; but had you not done as you have, you would have died a living death for treason against God, as he spoke to you in the depths of your own soul. Acting in obedience to the dictates of your conscience and the behests of your God, you have rendered yourself worthy the honor and glory of a gallows at the hands of slaveholders, who live, not merely as pirates do, to plunder and kill, but for a purpose far more cruel and inhuman — *i. e.*, to turn human beings into chattels.

Who would not thus render himself deserving a gallows at such hands? The highest honor Virginia or the Union can bestow on the champion of liberty, and the living resistant of slavery, is a gallows. From this day, let the friends of the slave march forth to battle with slavery, whether the conflict be on the domestic, social, religious, political or military arena, under the symbol of the gallows, with the martyr and champion of liberty hanging on it.

You must die, as to your corporeal existence. Your visible, tangible presence will no more inspire and urge us on to the conflict; but John Brown, the MAN, the defender of liberty, the assailant of slavery, and the friend of the slave, will live and be with us, to inspire us, to incite us, to spur us up and lead us on to a still closer and more resolute and deadly assault upon slaveholding. You die, conscious that by the gallows you have triumphed, and answered the one great end of your life more effectually than you would have done had you run off thousands of slaves. You triumph by the gallows, not by running off slaves. The nation is aroused. It must now meet slavery face to face, and see it in its deformity and its results. In every department of life, it must meet it and fight it, till it dies, and liberty is "proclaimed throughout all the land, to all the inhabitants thereof."

You, dear friend, whose memory will ever be precious, as that of the slaveholder will ever be detested, have kept your anti-slavery faith; you have fought a good fight, and may say, "Henceforth there is laid up for me a crown of glory, which the Lord, the righteous Judge, will give me in the day when the last slave shall be free. Now, Lord, lettest thou thy servant depart in peace, for mine eyes have seen thy salvation." Millions will follow thee, weeping, to the gallows. In pitying accents I hear thee say to them, "Friends of the slave! weep not for me, but weep for yourselves and your country; for in this conflict with slavery, there is not an

1 *

attribute of the Almighty that can take sides with the op-
pressor." Your execution is but the beginning of that death
struggle with slaveholders, which must end in striking the
last fetter from the last slave. On the scaffold, thou wilt
hear thy God, and the slave's God, saying unto thee, "Fear
not, for I am with thee; be not dismayed, for I am thy God;
I have chosen thee; thou art my servant; I will strengthen
thee; I will help thee; yea, I will uphold thee with the right
hand of my righteousness. All they that were incensed
against thee shall be ashamed and confounded; they shall
be as nothing; they that strive with thee shall perish; the
[anti-slavery] whirlwind shall scatter them." My spirit is
with thy spirit, in the dungeon and on the scaffold.

Thine, for the slave, and against the slaveholder, unto death,

HENRY C. WRIGHT.

THE above letter to John Brown, with the resolution passed
at Natick, November 20th, 1859, was forwarded to Gov.
Wise, of Virginia, accompanied with the following note, re-
questing him to deliver it to Capt. Brown, then in prison,
awaiting his execution :—

NATICK, Mass., Nov. 21st, 1859.

HENRY A. WISE, Governor of Virginia:

SIR,—Enclosed is a resolution adopted by the people of
Natick, Mass., the residence of the Hon. Henry Wilson. At
their request, I forward it to John Brown, with a letter to
him. The resolution and letter may give peace and satis-
faction to him in his last hours. However repulsive the
sentiments may be to you, and to the people over whom you
preside, they may sustain him on the scaffold. The appeal
is to your magnanimity and justice to put them into his
hands.

You think he has done foolishly and wickedly. We think
his object has been noble, and his motives disinterested,

heroic and sublime.   We ask not his life, but we do ask that
you would let him know that he lives, and ever will live, in
the hearts of his long-tried personal friends, and of the
friends of freedom and the enemies of slaveholding throughout the North.

Grant to us and to him this favor, and our sincere thanks
shall be yours, though our hearts must ever protest against
the injustice and political insanity that, for an effort so truly
humane, grand and heroic, shall consign his body to the
gallows.

Thine,

HENRY C. WRIGHT.

A copy of the letter to Brown, with the resolution passed
at Natick, November 20th, 1859, was also sent to Capt.
Avis, keeper of the jail in which Brown was confined, awaiting execution, with the following note : —

NATICK, Mass., Nov. 21st, 1859.

CAPTAIN AVIS:

SIR, — Pardon this intrusion by an utter stranger.   God
bless you for your kindness to John Brown in these, his last
hours !

If consistent with your feelings as a man, and your duties
as a jailor, you would oblige me by presenting the enclosed
to him for his perusal.   It is a resolution adopted by the citizens of Natick, Mass., as expressive of their views on a
subject now assuming paramount importance throughout the
North.   Though the sentiments of the resolution and of the
accompanying letter may be repugnant to you, it can do no
harm to allow your prisoner to read them, that he may stand
on the scaffold knowing that he is fully understood and appreciated by those who have known and sympathized with
his plans and movements the past few years, and that,
through his death, he will serve the cause he so much loves
more effectually, it may be, than he could have done by his
life.

God bless the single-hearted, grand and kingly man! He seems to us as one clothed with light and majesty as with a garment. Could he but be spared, there are thousands who would cheerfully take his place, and welcome the gallows in his stead. But he must die, as to corporeal existance, and in his death will consist his greatest triumph.

Thine,

HENRY C. WRIGHT.

LETTER TO THE RICHMOND ENQUIRER.

NATICK, Mass., Nov. 21st, 1859.

To THE EDITOR OF THE RICHMOND ENQUIRER : —

SIR, — A large and enthusiastic meeting of the citizens of this town (the residence of Hon. Henry Wilson) was held last evening, called to consider the following resolution : —

" Whereas, Resistance to tyrants is obedience to God ; therefore,
" Resolved, That it is the right and duty of the slaves to resist their masters ; and it is the right and duty of the people of the North to incite slaves to resistance, and to aid them in it."

This was adopted ; and though a United States Senator (Hon. Henry Wilson) and a United States Postmaster were present, not a dissentient voice was raised against it.

The resolution utters the thought of Massachusetts, of New England, and of New York. I have reason to know it does.

Insurrection, — resistance on the part of the slaves and of the North against slaveholders, — is the on e idea of the people. That insurrection is the right and duty of slaves, is he one controlling thought of the masses here. Though our Senators and Representatives in Congress dare not avow this as their opinion in Washington, at home, among their constituents, they countenance and sustain it by direct advocacy, or by silence. The North has reason to expect it of them, the coming session, that they will openly advocate the doctrine and practice of insurrection and resistance, as the right and duty of the slaves of the South and of the people of the non-slave States. We have much reason to hope, that, come what may, they will do it.

It was asserted in the above meeting, that John Brown, at Harper's Ferry, had truly embodied the general idea of the North, and had done no more than his simple duty to himself, to the slave, to the slaveholder, to his country, and his God. There are thousands among those who have known his plans and movements the past four or five years, and have sympathized with him, and who have known of his call, *as he believes*, from God, to do a deed that would arouse the South and the nation to consider the sin and danger of slavery, and who have known also of his unfaltering determination to do that deed, and strike that blow, who would now cheerfully take his place in the dungeon and welcome the gallows in his stead, if thereby he might be spared to lead on the mustering sons of liberty to free the slaves, and crush the power of those who live by whipping and selling women, and by " trafficking in slaves, and the souls of men."

The sin of this nation, as it was asserted in that meeting, is to be taken away, not by Christ, but by John Brown. Christ, as represented by those who are called by his name, has proved a dead failure, as a power to free the slaves. John Brown is and will be a power far more efficient. The nation is to be saved, not by the blood of Christ, (as that is now administered,) but by the blood of John Brown, which, as administered by Abolitionists, will prove the " power of God and the wisdom of God " to resist slaveholders, and bring them to repentance. John Brown and him hung will do that for the slaves and for those who enslave them which Christ and Him crucified has never been made to do. The blood of Christ, as dispensed by the American Church and clergy, has been the most nutritious aliment of American slavery, and has been made to add only to its growth and power; but the blood of Brown, as it will be dispensed by the friends of justice and humanity, will be its certain death, while it will add energetic life and resistless power to liberty.

Redemption is to come to the slave and his oppressors, not by the Cross of Christ, as it is preached among us, but by the gallows of Brown. The Cross of Christ — as borne aloft before this nation — has been and now is a bulwark of defence, a tower of strength, a munition of rocks, — THE GIBRALTAR of American slaveholders; the Gallows of Brown, as it will be borne aloft in front of the hosts of freedom — the true army of the living God against slavery — does and will strike terror to their hearts, and consternation into the ranks of slave-breeders and slave-traders, drive them from their strongholds, and make them a hissing and byword to all lands.

Henceforth, the slaves and their friends in the North will know nothing but John Brown and him hung; and they have only to shriek his name through the midnight chambers of repose of the merciless, but shivering, cowering, slave-drivers, to carry dismay to their guilty hearts. Slaveholders, and their allies and abettors, have known and will continue to know, nothing but Christ and him crucified, as they have learned Him from their slaveholding priests and churches; and they have raised and will continue to raise Him from the sepulchre of the dead past, only to sanctify "the sum of all villany," as embodied in themselves. John Brown and him hanged will be the inspiration and slogan of the aroused slaves and their friends, till the four millions, now held and used as chattels, bought and sold and herded together in concubinage as brutes, punished with death for every attempt to raise themselves to the condition of men and women, and compelled to feel after God and immortality amid beasts and creeping things, shall be regenerated and redeemed.

This may seem to you *madness*. It is so, as viewed from the slaveholding stand-point. But, it is the madness of the Good Samaritan and of Paul; it is the madness of Jesus Christ; the madness of one who sees and worships God in the *living*, rather than in the *dead*; in the living slave, rather than in a dead Jesus; in a living, rather than in a dead Christ. It is the madness of one who, on the public arena of life, by word and by deed, has sought to incite the slaves and the entire nation to a living, practical resistance to slaveholders, in every department of life, and who has taught the people of the North, for twenty-five years, that the purest, sublimest, and most acceptable worship they could render to the God of Justice and Liberty is — " TO BREAK EVERY YOKE, AND LET THE OPPRESSED GO FREE."

HENRY C. WRIGHT.

LETTER TO HENRY A. WISE,

WRITTEN ON THE DAY IN WHICH HE KILLED JOHN BROWN FOR

SEEKING TO GIVE FREEDOM TO SLAVES.

BOSTON, Friday, Dec. 2d, 1859.

To HENRY A. WISE, Governor of Virginia :

SIR,—This is the day and this the hour in which John Brown is being hanged by you. His dead body is now hanging on a gallows, and the eyes of twenty-five millions of this nation are fixed upon it. You erected that gallows, you dragged him to it, you tied that rope around his neck, you bound his hands and his feet, you drew that cap over his eyes, and having thus rendered him blind and helpless, you broke his neck.

At fifteen minutes past eleven o'clock, A. M., this day, you murdered John Brown! The entire nation saw you do it, and is a witness against you. Yourself, Virginia, and the nation, at this hour, adjudge you a murderer.

Why did you hang him? This is the one thought of the nation. You must answer it. How? You yourself have pronounced him one of "the truest, bravest, most sincere and noble" men you ever saw. You and your accomplices in this deed of blood assure us that the nation contained not a more " sincere, honest, heroic and conscientious man." Why, then, did you kill him?

Had he made an effort to rescue you, your wife and daughters, your mother and sisters from slavery and from the vengeance, the wrath, the rape and rapine of your slaves, would you have hung him? No. But he sought to rescue slaves from the wrath, rape and rapine of yourself and your fellow slave-breeders and slave-traders, and you killed him. Had he done for you and them the very deeds for which you have hung him, you and they would have pronounced him innocent, and crowned him with glory.

Your slaves have as good a right to enslave you, as you have to enslave them. They have as good a right to scourge your naked back, to drive you to unpaid toil, to sell you as a beast, to shoot you and tear you to pieces with bloodhounds, if you run away, as you have to do these things to them. They have as good a right to subject your wife and daughters, and your mother and sisters, to their passions, as you have to subject theirs to yours. They have as good a right to perpetrate robbery, murder, rape and rapine upon you and your confederates in slave-breeding and slave-trading, and upon your wives and children, as you have to perpetrate like outrages upon them. They have as good a right to defend themselves and families against you and your associates in plunder and rapine, as you have to defend yourselves against them. You and your co-workers in crime call on the North to come down and defend you and your families against your slaves. They come and defend you, and you thank them. The slaves call on John Brown to come down and deliver them and their families from your lusts and your cruelties, and defend their property, their liberties and lives against you. You say it is the duty of the North to defend you against the slaves. John Brown and his God told him it was his duty to defend the slaves against you. He came to Virginia to do so, and for doing his duty, you have hung him. Are you not a *murderer*?

What says Virginia of your deed? The slaves and all the world look on the seal with which, as Governor of the State, you stamp your letters and all public documents. What do they see? VIRGINIA, standing with one foot on the neck of a prostrate SLAVEHOLDER, whose head she has just cut off, and holding in her right hand the sword with which she did the deed, all reeking with his blood. Proud and exultant she stands, and in the consciousness of having done a meritorious deed, by ridding the world of a monster and Humanity of its most malignant foe, she challenges the homage of all for what she has done, and in her pride of victory exclaims:— *Sic semper tyrannis*—" Thus always deal with slaveholders"—*i. e.*, cut their heads off.

Thus Virginia, the State over which you are so proud to preside, says to your slaves, and to all slaves in the State, and in the United States, and in all the world—" CUT OFF YOUR MASTERS' HEADS." Not content with mere words, she *pictures* to them her own proud achievement, and calls on them to look at her in the very act of vanquishing her direst foe, and of beheading him ; thus *inciting* them, by an appeal to the eye as well as to the ear, to resistance, to insurrection, and to blood.

In her Constitution, Virginia says to her slaves, " You are born as free as are your masters, and have the same God-given right to your earnings, to yourselves, your wives, husbands, children and homes as they have." She is ever sounding in the ears of the slaves—" Give me liberty or give me death ! "—" Resistance to *slaveholders* is obedience to God." All the slaveholders and white men and women in Virginia are ever saying to the slaves, " If you, or any others, were to do unto us as we are daily and hourly doing unto you, we would kill, slay and destroy you. If we were in your places, we would kill every man, woman and child that should attempt to prevent us from getting and maintaining our freedom." Thus your State appeals to the slaves, to *incite* them to a bloody insurrection.

You, sir, make this appeal to the slaves, and to the people of the North. You flaunt this most ferocious and bloodthirsty prayer in their faces every time you set your official seal to a commission, a warrant, a draft, a law, or any document. By this act, your prayer to the slave is, " Arise ! and cut off the heads of all slaveholders ! "—and you invoke the North to come and help them. John Brown heard your prayer, and the prayer of Virginia. In answer to it, he came to Harper's Ferry. He there sought to rescue men and women from the condition of brutes and chattels, and to restore to them their God-given and State-acknowledged rights. He did not aim to do the bloody deed to slaveholders which

2

you and Virginia exhorted him to do — *i. e.*, BEHEAD THEM!
No; he was kind to the tyrants, to his own injury. He
simply sought to lead some slaves, imbruted by you and
your copartners in crime, to a land of freedom. By your
official seal and Constitution, and your historical reminis-
cences, you invited John Brown to come to Harper's Ferry
and run off slaves, and to kill all who should oppose him.
You and Virginia declared that it was the right and duty of
the slaves to rise against their masters, and to gain their
freedom by running away, or by beheading their oppressors;
and you told him it was his right and duty to help them.
John Brown came, with twenty-one assistants, to help him
in a work which you and all Virginia acknowledge would
have been a work of love, justice, and humanity, had it
been done to free you from slavery. You mustered the
State, called on the United States to hasten to your aid,
surrounded the self-forgetting hero and his little band, and
shot or hung them, deeming that you did a brave and
heroic act! You mustered the State and nation to the
defence of your property, your wives and children, your
houses and lives, against twenty-one men, who had no
thought of harm to you, but simply thought to give freedom
to slaves. Such bravery must, one day, be appreciated.
He was as innocent as were Washington, Lafayette, Franklin, Jefferson, Hancock, and Patrick Henry, and far more
deserving the approval of mankind. You took him, bound
him hand and foot, blindfolded him, and then broke his
neck! Yourself and Virginia being witnesses, are you not
a MURDERER? Verily, you have your reward!

Why have you and Virginia hung John Brown? To defend your property, (your slaves,) your liberty and lives,
against robbery and murder; and your wives and daughters,
your mothers and sisters, against rape and rapine. And
not being able to defend yourselves, you and Virginia called
on the United States to come and help you. You do, then,
hold that it is a right and duty to shoot and hang and behead
people in defence of liberty, life and home?

You, then, and Virginia, being witnesses, it is the right
and duty of the slaves to defend their earnings, their liberty
and lives, by arms and blood; and their wives and daughters against the rapine of their masters. You and your
fellow slave-breeders and slave-traders live by robbing

slaves of their labor, by invading their homes, and ravishing
their wives, daughters and sisters, and plundering their nur-
series and cradles; and by murdering them, if they attempt
to defend themselves and their families. So, in the very act
of hanging Brown to defend yourself, you justify him in
doing the deed for which you hang him!

Slaves of the South! People of the North! Look at the
commission of Judge Parker, who sentenced Brown to be
hung; look at the commission of General Taliaferro, who
heads the troops of Virginia and of the United States, now
surrounding the gallows on which hangs his murdered body;
open the commission of Captain Avis, the jailor, and of
Sheriff Campbell, who now stand by that murdered body!
Whose name is on all these?   Not that of Henry A. Wise,
Governor of Virginia. What seal is that?   VIRGINIA — her
foot on the prostrate and headless form of a slaveholder!

Once more: that DEATH-WARRANT! Look at it! The
name of Henry A. Wise is there.   What is the import of that
seal?   To the slaves it says: "Arise! Cut off your masters' heads! Kill, slay and destroy all who would enslave
you, or molest you in your efforts to secure your freedom!"
To John Brown it says, "Hasten to Harper's Ferry; incite the slaves to run away, and help them to exterminate
all who shall attempt to impede their exodus!"

Thus, in the very death-warrant under which Brown is
hung, you and Virginia pronounce him innocent of all evil,
and justify the very deed for which you hang him. In every
way, you pronounce him guiltless. Yet, you have hung
him! Are you not a murderer? Yes! Henry A. Wise and
Virginia being witnesses. Yes! the heart, the conscience,
the reason and history of the nation being witnesses. Yes!
by the testimony of mankind, and by the voice of God.

Dream not that John Brown will appear in this world's
history as "a fool," "a fanatic," "a robber," "a ruffian,"
"a madman," "a monomaniac," "a marauder," or "a
murderer." His plan was formed in wisdom and righteousness; and was executed in purest justice, goodness and
benevolence, according to the religion and government of
Virginia, and of the United States; and according to the convictions of ninety-nine out of every hundred of the people.

What was his object? To arouse the nation to consider
the sin, the shame, and the danger of slavery, with a view

to its abolition. What was his plan of action? RUNNING SLAVES OFF, or *dying* in the attempt. Either would answer his purpose. This he knew, and was prepared for the alternative. Death at your hands overtook him in the attempt, and when in the act of breaking his neck, your word was heard throughout the land, saying, "Surely, this is a just man!" Has he failed? Never was the life of man — death, rather — a more complete success.

What has been the one ruling thought of Virginia, and of every slave State, and of the Union, the past two months? John Brown and Harper's Ferry! What the one spoken and unspoken word of the entire nation? John Brown and Harper's Ferry! The one pulsation of the nation's heart has been, — John Brown and him hung, *for seeking to free slaves!* John Brown, *the friend of the slave*, has edited every paper, presided over every domestic and social circle, over every prayer, conference and church meeting, over every pulpit and platform, and over every Legislative, Judicial and Executive department of government; and he will edit every paper, and govern Virginia and all the States, and preside over Congress, guide its deliberations, and control all political caucuses and elections, for one year to come.

In a word, John Brown and him hung will be the one thought of the nation; and John Brown and him hung for "*bearing the yoke of the oppressed as if upon his own neck*," is now, and will continue to be, the one deep and humiliating feeling that will fill every heart with grief, sadness, shame, indignation and loathing. John Brown has triumphed; and that, too, according to his expectations, in death.

You have murdered him; but you, Virginia, and the nation, retire from the bloody deed a thousand-fold more impotent to defend slavery than you were before. You have murdered his body; but John Brown holds you, Virginia, the nation, and slavery, in his firm, determined grasp, more completely than he ever did before.

May John Brown and him hung be, to you, Virginia, and the nation, what Christ and him crucified was to his executioner, "A savor of life unto life, and not of death unto death!"

Thine, for eternal life to freedom, and a speedy death to slavery,

HENRY C. WRIGHT.

LETTER TO HON. HENRY WILSON,

TOUCHING THE NATICK RESOLUTION AND SERVILE RESISTANCE
AND INSURRECTION.

Boston, Dec. 10th, 1859.

Hon. Henry Wilson :

Sir,—In the Senate of the United States, you were called
upon, on Tuesday, December 6th, to give an account of
yourself to the slave-drivers for attending a meeting in
Natick, called to discuss a resolution affirming " the right
and duty of slaves to resist their masters, and the right and
duty of the North to aid them." A Mr. Brown asked you,
in an insolent tone — " Were you present to countenance
such a meeting ? " You explained and said, " It was a lecture attended generally by Democrats and others ; that no-
body interrupted the proceedings; that *only* some dozen
Garrison Abolitionists voted for the resolution, and that the
great mass of the meeting came from *curiosity.*" The
slave-driver who held the lash over you said, " I am satis-
fied ! " But another, Mr. Iverson, still flourished the lash
over you, taunting you because, " being a Senator from
Massachusetts, you heard such treasonable sentiments avowed
at a public meeting, in your own town, and did not at once
rebuke them, instead of sitting and giving silent assent to
them."

Instead of rebuking those insolent lords of the lash for
presuming to dictate to you your course of conduct at home,
among your neighbors, you submissively attempted to ex-
plain to them the whys and wherefors of your action, *out*
of Congress, as if anxious to deprecate their frowns and
stripes.

That meeting was called by public notice to discuss the
question of " Resistance to slaveholders as obedience to
God, in reference to John Brown at Harper's Ferry." It
was hoped and expected that both sides would be heard.
It was stated at the opening of the meeting, *you being present*, that it was not a lecture, but a meeting for discussion.
A prominent citizen of Natick was appointed chairman, who

2 *

introduced Mr. Wright, who read the resolution and com-
mented on it some forty minutes, and gave way. You (if I
mistake not, *by name*) were invited, with others, to give
your views for or against it, as your reason and conscience
should dictate. You declined, as was your right and duty,
if your own reason so decided. Though all would have
gladly heard you, none blamed you for your silence.

It was urged in that meeting, that it was the right and
duty of the slaves, and of the North, to embody their resistance to slaveholders in every department of life, wherever
they deemed it right to live — in domestic, social, ecclesiastical, political and commercial life; and that it was the right
of the slaves to defend themselves against the lusts, the
thefts, robbery and rapine of their masters, by arms and
blood, in the same sense that it is the right of the masters to
defend themselves against like outrages on the part of the
slaves.

As to military resistance, Mr. Wright denied that it was
ever *right* or *expedient*. At the same time, he said, if ever
it was right to resist tyrants by arms, it was the right and
duty of the slaves, and of the North, to resist slaveholders;
that if ever one human being deserved death at the hand of
another, (which Mr. Wright denied,) every slaveholder deserved it at the hand of the slave; and that, according to the
religion, the government, the popular opinion and universal
history of the nation, John Brown had done right, and only
his duty to God and Humanity, in resolving to run off slaves,
and to shoot down all who should oppose him in his God-
appointed work.

Three things were distinctly urged in that meeting, as
taught by the ministers, legislators, judges, presidents and
governors of the entire nation. (1) The right of slaves to
run away; (2) their right to defend themselves against all
who shall attempt to molest them; (3) their right to call on
the people of the North to aid them, and the duty of the
North to *incite* them to run away, and to defend them
against all, whether governmental officials or not, who shall
oppose their exodus.

It was urged upon Henry Wilson, Charles Sumner, William H. Seward, John P. Hale, and all Northern Senators
and Representatives, in and out of Congress, as a duty, to

incite slaves to insurrection and resistance of soul against slaveholders, and all who would enslave them. The hope was expressed that the slaveholders in Congress would bring Northern members to the test, that they might have an opportunity to affirm in Congress the sentiments they are known to entertain at home — *i. e.*, that it is the right and duty of slaves to seek freedom by running away, and to defend themselves against all who would intercept them, and that it is the right and duty of the North to *incite* and *aid* them thus to get their freedom.

Such sentiments were uttered in that meeting in your hearing, and not one word was said by you or any one against them. And it was said that your silence would be taken for consent. Why, then, do you intimate that you were silent because you did not wish " to *interrupt* the proceedings " ? You well know that, had you spoken, not one would have considered it an interruption. The feeling was that you were silent because your sense of justice, truth and humanity forbade you to oppose the resolution. I do not believe there were ten persons in the meeting who would have said that it is not right for slaves to run away, or that John Brown did not do right in inciting them to run away, and in helping to defend them against all who should oppose them.

It was not " curiosity," but sympathy with Brown, that brought them there. It would be difficult for you to convince your neighbors that it was not a deep interest in the life and fate of Brown that brought you there. It is true, as Iverson says, " by your silence, you gave your sanction to the resolution." You were invited to oppose it; you declined. Had you openly and earnestly sustained it, there were not probably ten in the hall, I doubt if there was one, who would not have admired you all the more for it.

I allude to this meeting, not because it is worthy of special notice in itself; for thousands like it are being held on the same subject all over the North, in which stronger sentiments, it may be, are urged without contradiction; but because you and other members of the Senate and of the House are trying to throw glamour in the eyes of Southern members, and make them think that Republicans have no sympathy with Brown and his efforts to run off slaves, and by so doing to arouse the nation to its great sin and danger. You would have them think that " regret and condemnation " of Brown and his objects are universal at the North. Well may they, in their terror and agony, ask you, " What mean those mighty gatherings, and that tolling of bells all over the North on the day of his execution ? What mean those speeches eulogistic of Brown and his doings, and so condemnatory of Wise, and Virginia, and their doings ? What means the almost universal applause bestowed on the remark of Ralph Waldo Emerson, the most prominent literary man, lecturer and moral philosopher in the nation, that the execution of the hero and saint of Harper's Ferry, ' Will make the gallows as glorious as the cross ' ? Why was it that the seizure, trial and execution of Brown, as a felon, swelled the Republican vote at the recent elections in the Northern States ? Will you, in the face of ten thousand facts like these, still assure the quaking slaveholders that Republicans have no sympathy with Brown ? Well may they retort upon you — " You take a queer way to show it."

Please show the doings of the Massachusetts Legislature on the day of the execution (Friday, December 2d) to the slaveholders, and tell them that is evidence of the truth of your remarks ! What were they ? In the Senate, soon as the session was opened, Mr. Luce, of the Island District, moved, " That, in view of the execution of John Brown in Virginia, the Senate do now adjourn." This motion was negatived — ayes, 8 ; nays, 11. At 12, noon, Mr. Luce again moved, " That, as it was probably about this time that John Brown was being executed in Virginia, as an expression of sympathy for him, the Senate do now adjourn." A debate ensued.

" MR. ODIORNE, of Suffolk, expressed admiration for Brown as a man; declaring that he had the greatest sympathy with him."

" MR. WALKER, of Hampden, said he yielded to no man in sympathy for Brown. He looked at the action of Virginia as unjust, and condemned the unseemly haste with which the trial and execution had been hurried forward."

" MR. DAVIS, of Bristol, did not propose to condemn the acts of Brown, as he wished them to be judged by posterity ;

and he felt sure that *no more heroic or brighter name would be found in history, than that of old Osawatomie Brown.* Brown, with the Constitution of the United States in one hand, and the Golden Rule in the other, marched straight forward and attacked the Slave Power, and he was to be honored for it."

" Mr. WALKER, of Hampden, said he did not believe, as a lawyer, that John Brown had been legally convicted of treason or murder. While he did not wish to go into the slave States to run off slaves himself, yet he did not object to others doing it in any way they saw fit."

" Mr. HOTCHKISS, of Franklin, said he was a States' Rights man, in the fullest sense ; but he thought it would be as perfectly proper to adjourn out of sympathy for Brown as for any other great and good man ; and he considered John Brown *one of the noblest works of God.* If Brown had done wrong, it was an error of the head, and not of the heart. He held the Governor of Virginia guilty of wilful murder, and this act would be the hanging of the Governor and of the whole State of Virginia. Brown had not been proved guilty."

On this second motion, the vote was — yeas, 12 ; nays, 20. Such was the spirit and action of the Senate. But one spoke condemnatory of Brown and his deeds. Remember, the Senate is almost entirely Republican. All who spoke in favor of Brown were such. Read the above, and then tell the slaveholders that Republicans have no sympathy with Brown, and no responsibility for his deeds ! What will they think of you ? Would that Republicans would avow their work and glory in it ; for this is the richest fruit they have ever borne, — so far as it is theirs.

In the House, at the opening of the session, Mr. RAY, of Nantucket, — moved " That, for the great respect we have for the truthfulness and faith that John Brown has in man and his religion, and the strong sympathy for the love of liberty (the avowed principle of Massachusetts) for which he is this day to die, this House do now adjourn."

" Mr. ROBINSON, of Middleboro', was unwilling to say John Brown was right, though he respected him, and thought his motives good."

" Mr. Griffin, of Malden, said, the spirit of the order is merely a tribute to the piety and integrity of John Brown. Let us imitate old Brown, and attend to the business God and our constituents have given us to do. He had his views of John Brown and of his value to the race ; but this was not the place to express them. In other places, it might be done."

It was done in a meeting of three thousand in the Tremont Temple, that very night, — called for the purpose of express-ing sympathy for Brown, and abhorrence of his murder by the Governor of Virginia.

In this meeting, S. E. Sewall, a much respected lawyer of Boston, and a leading Republican, said : — " Under these circumstances, whether John Brown was technically guilty of any offence against the laws of Virginia or not, he had not had a fair trial, and his execution is therefore BUTCHERY and MURDER, and the Judge and Governor were only the tools of Virginia in carrying out this JUDICIAL ASSASSINA-TION. As it is, Governor Wise seems likely to be pilloried by history at the side of Pontius Pilate, as the man who shed innocent blood in violation of his own convictions of right, to satisfy the clamor of a deluded populace, crying, " Crucify him ! crucify him !'"

Mr. Griffin, at the same meeting, said : " He undertook to defend Pontius Pilate against a comparison with Governor Wise. The chairman should apologize to the memory of Pontius Pilate for the comparison." (Uproarious applause.)

With such facts before them, what must the slaveholding Senators think of your assertion, that Brown and his deeds excite only " regret and condemnation " among Republi-cans ? Brown, Iverson, Mason, and all the Senators from the South, justly tremble for themselves, their wives and their children. They frankly declare to you and to the nation their terror and agony. They say the North sympathizes with Brown and his deeds, and in so doing seeks to incite in-surrection, rebellion, and resistance among their slaves. It is true. Their fears are well founded. Why seek to lull them into security till the storm shall burst upon them in a way they dream not of, — as it surely will, and deluge their homes and their plantations with blood, unless they escape by repentance and emancipation? Why should you seek to quiet their guilty consciences and awakened terrors?

The masses of the North are in sympathy with Brown and his deeds. In no State is this more true than in that which you represent. In no place in the State is that sympathy more vital than in your own immediate neighborhood; as if your presence there had only tended to kindle the flame and keep it blazing.

Millions in the North rejoice that the slaveholders in Congress bring you and all your associates in politics to this one test, — *i. e.*, *Is resistance to slaveholders the right and duty of the slaves and of the North*? Will you and your fellow-Republicans help to kill the slaves if they attempt to defend themselves, their wives and children against the rape, rapine, robbery and murder perpetrated on them, daily, by their masters; or will you side with the slaves against the masters? Was John Brown a traitor against God and humanity? Henry Wilson and Charles Sumner will never say he was.

Slaveholders may well turn pale with terror. As Iverson and Mason say, "they sleep on the brink of a volcano." They know they deserve death, *on their own showing*, at the hands of their slaves. They feel, hourly, their victim's knife at their throats; his dagger at their hearts, and his torch at their dwellings; and their wives and daughters outraged by those whose wives and daughters, mothers and sisters, they themselves have ravished. If they will persist in turning men and women into brutes and chattels, they must abide the results of their inhuman deeds. Their reward is sure and terrible. The bayonets of the North will not much longer defend them. I would that you and your associates in Congress were as true to liberty as the South is to slavery; that you would, in every department of life, as truly embody resistance to slavery, as they do resistance to liberty. Then this "irrepressible conflict" would soon be ended; and the HIGHER LAW be the *only* rule of action, *in* Congress as well as *out* of it. For the Constitution and the enactments of Congress are but so much blank paper, and will be set at nought as such, when they are opposed to that HIGHER LAW which enjoins it upon slaves to escape from slavery, and upon the North to incite and help them to escape. If this be treason — as it unquestionably is — against the LOWER LAW, and you and your fellow-Republicans undertake to hang all such traitors, as you say you will, rest assured you will have enough to do. You must, indeed, become a COMMON hangman.

Judged from the stand-point of the religion and government of this nation, the design of John Brown was founded in the deepest wisdom and benevolence, and executed with consummate skill, and unrivalled heroism, integrity, and self-forgetfulness. His life was a complete success ; his death, an unparalleled and most honorable triumph. He sought to arouse the *soul* of this nation, the intellect, the conscience, the sympathy and will, to a state of resistance, rebellion, insurrection against slaveholders, and against every law, Constitution, Bible or religion that sanctions and sustains them in turning men, women, and children into beasts and chattels. He sought to accomplish this chief end of his existence by running off slaves or by death. He has triumphed by the gallows ! The blood of John Brown appeals to God and Humanity against slaveholders and their confederates in crime. To that appeal, the heart of this nation and of the civilized world will respond, in one defiant shout, " RE-SISTANCE TO SLAVEHOLDERS IS OBEDIENCE TO GOD !"

HENRY C. WRIGHT.

LETTER TO WM. LLOYD GARRISON,

TOUCHING REBELLION AND INSURRECTION AGAINST SLAVEHOLDERS.

BOSTON, Dec. 11th, 1859.

DEAR GARRISON:

I use the words resistance, rebellion, and insurrection, because these alone can truly express those mental, social and moral conditions which God and Humanity enjoin in regard to slaveholders.

Thirty years ago, the soul of this nation was in a condition of cowering subserviency to that power which turns every sixth man, woman and child into " a chattel personal." Reason, conscience, sympathy and will had succumbed, and apparently had lost the capacity to rise in rebellion against it. Insurrection against slave-breeders seemed not only an impossibility, but an immorality ; a kind of blasphemy against what was considered a God-ordained and time-honored practice. Slavery was inter-blended with all domestic, social, ecclesiastical, political and commercial relations, and defended by the religious, governmental and military power. Wherever men and women lived, there they embodied a living submission to slaveholders. Resistance, or insurrection against them, in any relation, in thought, feeling, word or deed, was counted a felony against the peace of society, against the Union, and its sovereign power.

Four millions of slaves, this day, are, by reason of the influence that is brought to bear upon them, made to believe and feel that the greatest sin they can commit, the sin most sure to make them liable to the vengeance and lash of their oppressors, and to all " the miseries of this life, to the wrath of God and the pains of hell forever," is that of insurrection and resistance against slaveholders, in thought, word or deed. Their will-power to resist is gone. They have *no will* of their own ! To have a will, a conscience, or an aversion to their enslavement, and to express it in word or deed, instantly subjects them to the lash or the gallows. The will of the tyrant is their only legalized and baptized rule of life.

3

Thirty years ago, the entire North, in its domestic, social, religious, political, commercial and military life, was in the same state of abject subserviency to slaveholders. The people seemed not only to have lost the power to resist them, but actually to feel honored that slave-breeders and slave-catchers counted them worthy to do their work of shame and infamy. The very life of their souls to resist seemed to have become extinct. So far as insurrection against them was concerned, the nation was dead and buried in an ignominious grave of servile submission.

You, in 1830, sounded the tocsin of insurrection and revolution against slaveholders, and all that sustains them. In the name of God and Humanity, you proclaimed war against the nation's protected and colossal crime. You said that you would be heard; that you would not yield; that you would never turn back; that you or slavery must die. You struck for *immediate, unconditional* abolition. What was the first work to be done? To arouse the people of the North, and place them in an attitude of insurrection against slaveholders, in thought, feeling, word, and deed; to incite them to irreconcilable hostility to " the highest kind of theft, *i. e.*, man-stealing," and to the injustice, robbery, rape and rapine inherent in slavery. The reason, conscience, moral and social nature and will of the North were to be quickened and brought into a state of inexorable, undying rebellion against slaveholders, *as such*. The people of the North, in the family and social circle, in the church, at the ballot-box, in the market, and in all places where they think it their right and duty to live, were to be made to regard and treat slaveholders as they do burglars, thieves, robbers, murderers, midnight assassins, and ravishers of helpless innocence, and to feel that, as such, they have no right to breathe God's air, to see his light, or to *live* in his universe ; that, *as slaveholders*, they have no rights which *any man* is bound to respect. This was the first work to be done. By appeals to reason, conscience, pity, and sympathy, made through the press and the living lecturer and speaker, despite the efforts of the Church and State to lull their souls to quietness, life was infused into multitudes in behalf of the slave.

You called on the people of the North to gird on the armor of God against slaveholders. Resistance, rebellion, insurrection against them, and all that sustains them, in sentiment, in principle, in spirit, word and deed, was the watchword of the Anti-Slavery Movement. Insurrection was couched in the very name by which the enterprise was christened, *i. e.*, ANTI-SLAVERY. An Anti-Slavery *soul*, and an Anti-Slavery *life*, were to be created in the North ; which meant a soul and a life, an interior and exterior life, rebellious and insurrectionary against slaveholders. The souls of the Northern people were to be aroused to cease to side with the oppressors against the oppressed, (as they had ever done,) and to yield up reason and conscience, and all their sympathy, and all their powers of soul and body, to the slaves against their enslavers. Two positions were established : (1) That it is the right and duty of the enslaved and the free to resist all attempts to hold and use human beings as chattels. (2) That it is our right and duty to use all such means to free the slaves as we would use to free ourselves, if we were slaves.

These two positions were, and have been to this day, maintained by you, by Adin Ballou, by Wendell Phillips, and by all Abolitionists. " Incite the slaves to escape from slavery, and defend them against the rape, rapine, and atrocities of those who would enslave them, by the same weapons with which you would defend yourselves, your wives and children. Resist slave-catchers, in behalf of the *black* slaves, by the same means that you would use in behalf of *white* slaves." This has been the uniform teaching of Abolitionists from the beginning. Every paper, every letter, every speech, every prayer, every exhortation, has been designed to bring the souls of the people into a state of insurrection against slaveholders, and an argument to induce them to use all such means as they would use, or wish others to use, for their own protection.

As to *armed* or *military* resistance to slaveholders, or to ANY evil-doers, my soul has ever resisted it, and ever must, as inexpedient, unjust and inhuman. Life or liberty can never be protected by killing men. MAN-KILLING is the basis of MAN-STEALING. Human liberty can never be made sacred by the taking of human life. Respect for liberty can never result from contempt for life. Liberty will be safe, only as life is reverenced. The inviolability of life is the only foundation of absolute safety to liberty.

Such has been my cherished conviction for thirty years, as it has been yours. It is because human governments are founded on the right to kill men, in violence and murder, and on that revengeful doctrine of " blood for blood," that I have never taken any part in their administration, by voting, or otherwise. I have no more respect for the authority of the General or State governments, than for that of the wolf or hyena. To me, they are all, as now constituted, but " covenants with Death, and agreements with hell." These governments, in their essential spirit, principles and practices, are a deliberate and formal rejection of those sacred and only truths that are absolutely conservative of " Life, Liberty and Happiness," *i. e.,* — " Love your enemies," " Forgive as you would be forgiven," " Return to no man evil for evil, but overcome evil with good." They all ignore the spirit and life of the Martyr of Calvary. And the one deep anguish of my heart, as I look on the martyr of Harper's Ferry, is, that his hands, ever so faithful to lib- to liberty, are stained with a brother's blood.

But while this is " the way, the truth and the life " to me, ninety and nine out of every hundred of the enslaved and enslavers, North and South, politicians and priests, *in their own defence,* insist that *armed* resistance to slavehold- ers is obedience to God ; and that it is the right and duty of the enslaved to defend themselves, their wives and daugh- ters, against the cruelties, the rape and rapine of their en- slavers, by arms and blood ; and to kill, slay and destroy all who invade their homes, to drag the objects of their affection to the auction-block, to be sold like brutes. In their own case, they hold that, if they were slaves, it would be the right and duty of John Brown, and of all freemen, to help them to insurrection. I hold them responsible to their own accepted laws of life, to use the same means to defend the Southern slaves, and their wives and children, which they would use, or wish others to use, to defend themselves. I would say to the people of the North : " Go, *incite* slaves to run away, and guide them on their way to Canada, as John Brown proposed to do ; and if slaveholders or their ecclesiastical and political minions attempt to oppose them, and to re-enslave them, defend them, as Brown proposed to do, by the same weapons you would use were you, and your

• wives and children, the fugitives. Rouse the slaves to rebellion and insurrection, and put into their hands *only* such weapons as you would.use in your own behalf, were you insurgent slaves. If you deem it wrong to use deadly weapons to defend yourselves, do not defend the slaves in that way; but if you would deem the torch and sabre justifiable means of insurrection in your own behalf, were you slaves, use the same in behalf of Southern slaves."

But the people of the North have been in sympathy with, and have plighted their faith and their power to, the enslavers, rather than the enslaved. While, in every possible way, from the pulpit, the platform, the press, they proclaimed armed resistance and armed insurrection against slaveholders as the right and duty of all *white* people, they have urged a meek, humble, unreasoning, uncomplaining and abject submission on the part of the *black* slaves. The *white* slaveholders perpetrate robbery, rape and rapine upon *black* slaves and their wives and daughters, and if the black slaves strike those *white* ravishers dead, Edward Everett, and the nation, sustain these Christian and Anglo-Saxon man-stealers in their " midnight and merciless atrocities, and their abominations, not to be named by *Christian* lips to *Christian* ears," and hang and shoot the outraged slaves for resisting them. But, if the black slaves return to these white plunderers and ravishers of their homes, *according to their deeds,* instantly Edward Everett begins to talk of " midnight burnings, wholesale massacres, merciless tortures, and deeds too unutterably atrocious for the English language." Before God and eternal justice and truth, whatever it is right for the *white* enslavers to do to *black* slaves and their wives, daughters, mothers and sisters, it is right for *black* slaves to do to their *white* enslavers and their wives, daughters, mothers and sisters. Whatever the people of the North would help the *white* slaveholders to do to their *black* slaves, they should, and will, one day, help the *black* slaves to do to the *white* slaveholders.

Let the North cut loose from their bloody alliance with slaveholders, imitate John Brown, and form a league of offence and defence with the slaves against their enslavers. Let them do in defence of freedom to the slaves whatever they would do in defence of their own freedom. Let the

3 *

North use all their power to give liberty to the slaves, which they would use to secure freedom to themselves. If they would use the torch and sabre to obtain and secure freedom to themselves, let them use the same weapons to give freedom to the slaves of Virginia.

Now they are politically, not morally, bound to aid slaveholders in their unprovoked, inhuman and murderous assault upon the slaves and their defenceless wives and children, and to shoot down the slaves if they attempt resistance or insurrection. Let them from this hour make an everlasting covenant with the slaves and the slaves' God, to *incite* and *aid* them to rebellion against man-stealers; and incite them to insurrection, and defend them against all who would crush them back into slavery, by all such means as they would use to defend themselves. This is what God and Humanity demand of every man and woman in the North, and in the world.

Subjection to an outward, arbitrary authority is the basis of chattel slavery, and of all oppression. The power of the Church and State, the consuming wrath, the lash, the bowie-knife, the revolver, the rifle and bloodhound of slaveholders, and their allies, and the vengeance and terror of an Almighty God, are brought to bear on the ignorant, cowering slaves, to crush out the last vestige of their manhood, and bring them into an unresisting, unreasoning, humble submission to that arbitrary, bloody power that enslaves them. The souls of the slaves fall prostrate, having no will of their own, and deeming every rebellion, insurrectionary thought and feeling, a crime deserving scourging and death, and eternal banishment from God and heaven. The mission of anti-slavery is to inspire them with rebellious thoughts and feelings, and incite them to insurrectionary words and deeds (not deeds of violence and blood) against their inhuman and godless masters.

So that same power of Church and State, the fierce wrath and threatened vengeance of slave-breeders, and the entire power of the government and religion of the nation, and the terrors of death, judgment and eternity, have been brought to bear on the people of the North, to compel them into humble subserviency to the Slave Power. You and your coadjutors have long labored to incite the cowering and crushed souls of the people of the North to a living, practical insurrection against that power; to arouse them to thoughts and feelings, to words and deeds of undying hostility against all constitutions and bibles, all religions and governments, and all men and women, that enslave human beings, or that teach submission on the part of slaves to the power that enslaves them.

The prestige of the words " rebellion " and " insurrection," " rebel " and " insurgent," " treason " and " traitor," for purposes of oppression, as a means to palsy and cower the soul into subserviency to slaveholders, and to constitutions, laws, bibles and religions that sustain them, was fast disappearing before the anti-slavery movement. The gallows and blood of Brown have about dissolved the charm altogether. Rebellion, insurrection and treason against slaveholders, and every authority and influence that sustains them, are fast coming to be expressive of our highest allegiance to God and Humanity. They are coming to be consecrated and holy words, and significant only of justice, honor, fidelity, love, and of whatever is beautiful, grand and heroic in human nature.

The whole power of the Church is wielded to overawe the souls of the people, and bring them submissively and abjectly to yield to the authority of their creed, and without one resisting or rebellious thought or feeling to do its behests, however inhuman they may be, even to turning men and women into chattels, or hanging them on a gallows. The Bible, the only authority in religious faith and practice, and insurrection against it a sin unto eternal death — this is the sentiment and history of the American Church.

The power of the Union and General Government, and of the politics and military of the country, is brought to bear to subject the people to the authority of their Constitution, their political creed; and rebellion, insurrection, treason against that in thought, feeling, word or deed, is counted the sin of sins, and to be expiated only on the gallows; the Constitution the only authority in social, commercial, civil and political life; and resistance and treason against it a sin unto death! For resisting that authority, by attempting to give freedom to those who by it were pronounced slaves, John Brown is hung, and a national gallows awaits all who have enough justice, humanity and piety to imitate him.

Edward Everett dooms slaves to death, who dare to resist the " midnight and merciless atrocities, the wholesale murders, and the abominations not to be spoken by Christian lips to Christian ears," that are perpetrated upon them and their wives and children by Christian hands; that pimp and pander to the lusts of slave-breeders, glorifies them for committing those atrocities, " too unutterable for the English language," upon the slaves and their helpless families, but hangs the slaves and their friends who incite and aid them to resistance and defence!

Abject, humble, uncomplaining submission to external, arbitrary authority, is the law and gospel of Church and State; even when that authority counts manhood and womanhood, female virtue, conjugal fidelity, the purity of marriage, and the sanctity of parentage, crimes punishable with death.

God and Humanity call the slaves of the South and the people of the North to insurrection and treason against a power so Satanic in spirit, and so rapacious, so libidinous, so malignant and murderous in practice. INSURRECTION OF SOUL against slaveholders, the right and duty of slaves and of the North — this is the first step; then, the means of resistance are to be such, only, as we would use in our own behalf, were we slaves.

The slaveholders have hung John Brown. Let them be assured there are tens of thousands of John Browns now hovering on the confines of slavery, ready to enter in and scatter themselves all over the South, to incite slaves to insurrection against their masters, and to guide them on their way to Canada, bidding defiance to slaveholders, and all slaveholding and slave-catching constitutions and laws; being ready to meet the alternative of a slaveholder's gallows. That instrument of torture has lost its terrors. IT IS THE RIGHT AND DUTY OF SLAVES TO GAIN AND DEFEND THEIR FREEDOM. IT IS THE RIGHT AND DUTY OF THE PEOPLE OF THE NORTH TO INCITE AND HELP THEM TO FREEDOM. This is becoming a paramount duty in the estimation of thousands, and no terrors of the slaveholder's wrath and vengeance will prevent them from doing it.

HENRY C. WRIGHT.

APPENDIX.

SPEECH OF HON. HENRY WILSON,

At an Anti-Slavery Festival held in Cochituate Hall, Boston, on the evening of January 24th, 1851, to celebrate the completion of the twentieth year of the existence of "The Liberator."

From the Boston "Liberator" of Jan. 31, 1851.

MR. CHAIRMAN, AND LADIES AND GENTLEMEN:

I suppose the reason why you, Mr. Chairman, who have the good fortune to preside over this joyous festival of the friends of liberty, assembled here to-night, have called upon me, is because I have the good fortune, or perhaps the misfortune, to preside over one branch of the "assembled wisdom" of the "great and General Court." On taking the chair, sir, you quoted the words of the great dramatist, that "some men were born great, some achieved greatness, and others have greatness thrust upon them." Now, sir, surrounded as you are, on either hand, by men who "were born great," and by men who have "achieved greatness," I am surprised, and this audience will be more surprised, that you should call upon one who has simply had "greatness thrust upon" him, to mar the festivities of this occasion, by inflicting a speech upon those who have been charmed by the glowing eloquence of the gifted and brilliant orators [Mr. Thompson and Mr. Phillips] who have addressed us. Our friend Phillips said, that he wished "to have a little scream from every one." You must, sir, have acted upon that hint in calling upon me. [Laughter.]

At a late hour this afternoon, I learned that the friends of freedom were to have a meeting here to-night, in honor of William Lloyd Garrison. I am here to-night, sir, to express my love for the great cause your guest has advocated for twenty years through the columns of the *Liberator*, [hear hear!] and my profound admiration and respect for his sel, sacrificing and unfaltering devotion to it, amid obloquy and reproach. It is my misfortune, perhaps, to differ from him on many important questions. Differing, however, from him as I do, I have ever honored him for his unshrinking zeal and unwavering fidelity to the cause of liberty and progress. [Applause.] For twelve years I have read the *Liberator ;* and, sir, if I love liberty, and loathe slavery and oppression, if I entertain a profound regard for the rights of man all over the globe, I owe it, in a great degree, to the labors of William Lloyd Garrison. [Prolonged applause.] I am not ashamed to acknowledge the debt of gratitude I owe him for his labors in behalf of three millions of men, and no fear of censure, ridicule or reproach shall deter me from expressing, on all fit and proper occasions, my respect and admiration for the man. [Applause.] Sir, the unceasing labor he has given to the cause of liberty and humanity for these twenty past years will cause his name and his memory to be cherished and revered ages after the stone which shall lie upon his grave shall crumble and mingle with the dust. [Hear! hear!] And when that great day comes, as surely it will come, — for God reigns, — when three millions of men, held in slavery in this republic, shall be free, the friends of liberty will acknowledge, what many now deny, the patriotism of William Lloyd Garrison. [Cheers.]

I came here, also, to-night, sir, to listen to the voice of one of the most gifted orators of the old world, whose eloquent tones are still ringing in our ears. You have alluded, Mr. Chairman, to the jealous feelings of our countrymen to foreign interference. Sir, I am an American — with American sympathies, feelings, and prejudices. I love my country, with all her faults, with a supreme devotion. I go for my country now, at all times, and on all occasions, and in every contest. Sir, I love not England. [Sensation.] I am not dazzled by her splendor or awed by her power, although the sun never goes down on her possessions, and her flag floats over her citadels of power in the four quarters of the globe, and upon every sea. But, sir, I honor the friends of liberty and progress in England, whose efforts for the last thirty years, in the cause of human progress, have never been surpassed by the efforts of any class of men in any portion of the civilized world. [Hear! hear!] Yes, sir, I undertake to say here, to-night, that in no part of the world, and in no age of the world, and by no race in the world, have greater efforts been made for human progress and human liberty, than have been made during the last thirty years in Old England. [Applause.] Her reformers have achieved the most brilliant victories. Among all her brilliant intellects, who have linked their names with the great ideas of Progress, no name shines more brightly than the name of George Thompson. [Applause.] As an American, loving the good name of my native land, jealous of its honor and its fame, I have felt the deepest mortification, that in the city of Boston, in old Faneuil Hall, the man who has stood up fearlessly in England and supported American principles, and defended the American name, should be received by men, calling themselves American Democrats, with ridicule and denunciations. [Applause.] His name is indissolubly linked with those great measures of reform which have for their object the elevation and improvement of the people of England. His voice has been raised in behalf of the millions of British India; and for West India emancipation, — the noblest act in the annals of British history, — his labors were freely given. His labors have been such, since he left our shores fifteen years ago, as should have given him, in Faneuil Hall and every where, a warm and hearty welcome. [Applause.] And, sir, as an American, loving my country, cherishing the great fundamental principles on which its institutions are founded, I come here to-night, and give him the same cordial welcome to America, that I would extend to the men who have nobly struggled on the lost fields where Liberty has been cloven down. [Sensation.] And as he may be called upon in a few months to leave us, I trust that when he goes, there will be none, at least in Massachusetts, who will censure him for laboring to blot from our country the sin and shame of slavery. [Much enthusiasm.]

Sir, allusion has been made to-night to the small begin-
nings of the great anti-slavery movement, twenty years ago,
when the *Liberator* was launched upon the tide. These
years have been years of devotion and of struggles unsur-
passed in any age or in any cause. But, notwithstanding
the treachery of public men, notwithstanding the apostacy
for which the year 1850 was distinguished, I venture to say,
that the cause of liberty is spreading throughout the whole
land, and that the day is not far distant when brilliant victories for freedom will be won. We shall arrest the exten-
sion of slavery, and rescue the Government from the grasp
of the Slave Power. We shall blot out slavery in the National Capital. We shall surround the slave States with a
cordon of free States. We shall then appeal to the hearts
and consciences of men, and in a few years, notwithstanding
the immense interests combined in the cause of oppression,
we shall give liberty to the millions in bondage. [Hear!
hear!] I trust that many of us will live to see the chain
stricken from the limbs of the last bondman in the republic!
But, sir, whenever that day shall come, living or dead, no
name connected with the anti-slavery movement will be
dearer to the enfranchised millions than the name of your
guest — William Lloyd Garrison. [Prolonged applause.]

Such were the sentiments of Henry Wilson in 1851.
Are they not his sentiments to-day?